magic

wand

spell

Spell

broomstick

cauldron

witch

wizard

Gingerbread man

castle

dragon

prince

princess

contents

Picture word book

compiled by LYNNE J BRADBURY
illustrated by LYNN N GRUNDY

Ladybird Books Loughborough

This collection of words is about children and their environment. The book presents words children use, words they see around them and the words for objects with which they are familiar.

Each object or scene is illustrated using simple, bold, full colour pictures. The book is arranged by subject and not alphabetically so that, for example, a child wanting the word kettle will find that word in the kitchen scene.

Very young children will enjoy talking about the pictures with an adult and having the objects named for them. Older children will be able to use the book as reference for their reading and writing as well as for enjoyment.

An alphabetical index is provided at the back of the book to assist the parent or teacher.

Girl   Boy

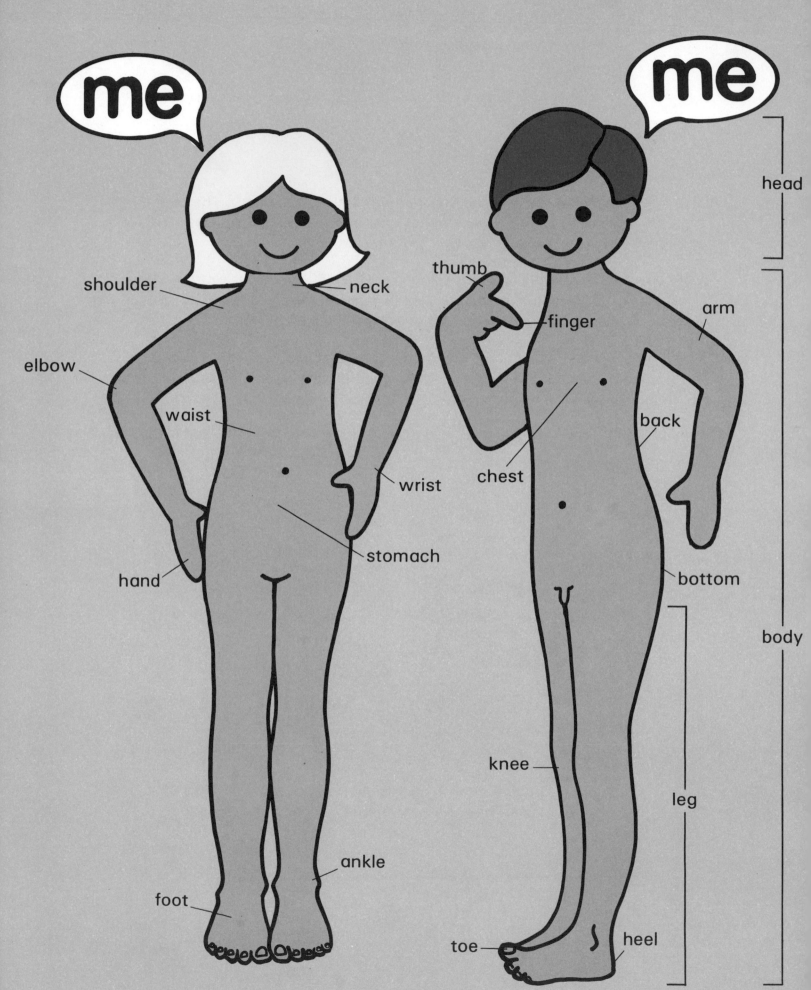

2

hair

nose

chin

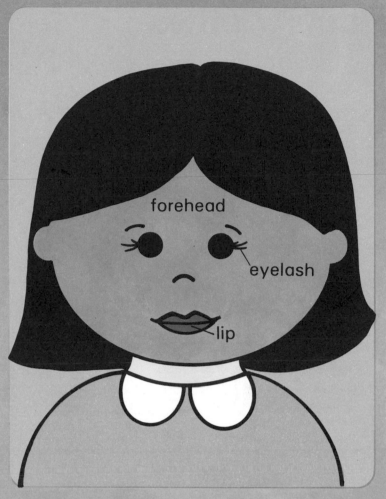

forehead

eyelash

lip

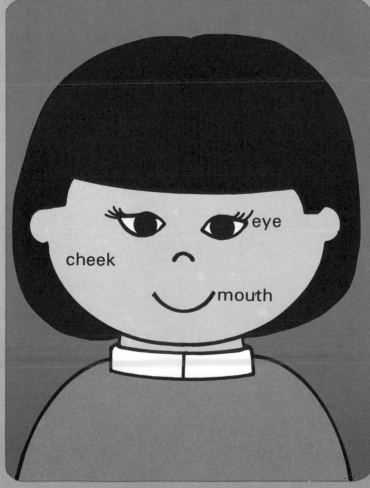

eye

cheek

mouth

eyebrow

ear

nostril

Clothes

indoor clothes

blouse

shirt

tie

skirt

jeans

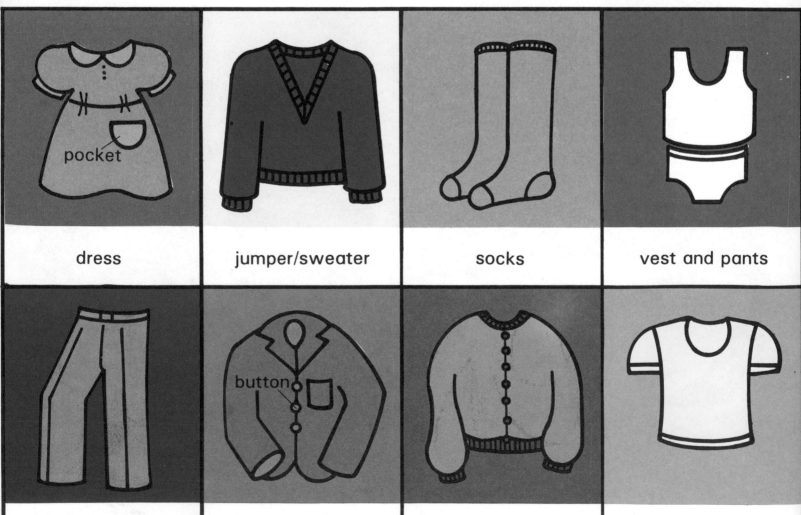

pocket	
dress	jumper/sweater

socks

vest and pants

button

| trousers | blazer/jacket | cardigan | tee shirt |

4

outdoor clothes

hat

coat

wellingtons

mackintosh/raincoat

laces

shoes

gloves

zip

anorak

scarf

night clothes

pyjamas

dressing gown

nightdress/ nightie

slippers

5

Family

mother/
mum/
mummy

aunt/
auntie

father/
dad/
daddy

brother

baby

uncle

grandmother/
grandma/
granny/
nanna/
nanny

grandfather/
grandad/
grandpa

sister

cousin

brother

7

Home

flats

chimney

house

roof

tiles

gutter

window

drainpipe

window

window sill

porch

bell

front door

keyhole

letterbox

step

gate

bricks

wall

hedge

path

8

Living room/Lounge

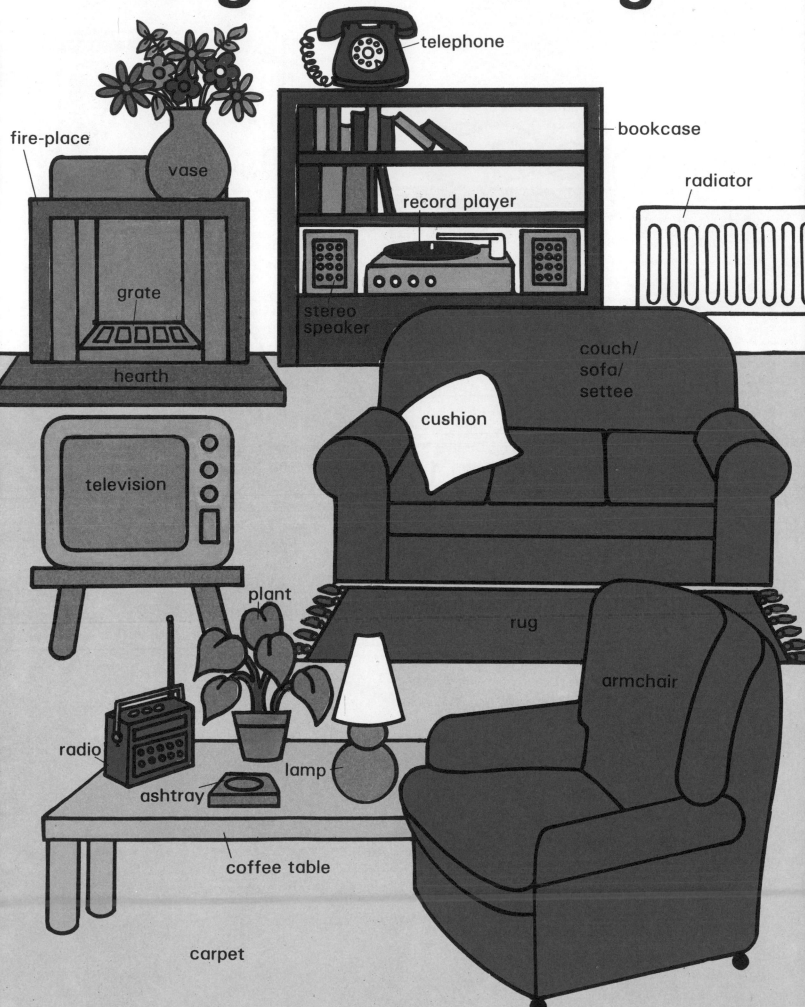

telephone

bookcase

fire-place

radiator

vase

record player

grate

stereo
speaker

hearth

couch/
sofa/
settee

cushion

television

plant

rug

armchair

radio

lamp

ashtray

coffee table

carpet

Dining room

picture

teapot

cup

saucer

tray

fruit bowl

sideboard

chair

fork

plate

water jug

knife

spoon

glass

table-mat

pepper

salt

tablecloth

Kitchen

fish slice

ladle

sieve

grill

spice rack

taps

washing-up bowl

draining board

pan

sink

frying pan

drawer

cupboard

oven

tea towel

cooker

rolling pin

iron

freezer

kettle

plug

mixer

refrigerator/ fridge

washing machine

pedal bin

stool

dustpan

brush

vegetable rack

Bedroom

light

wardrobe

coathanger

rail

mirror

comb

brush

dressing table

pillow

blanket

sheet

bed

bedspread

teddy bear

carpet

continental quilt/ duvet

alarm clock

book

hot water bottle

bedside table

Bathroom

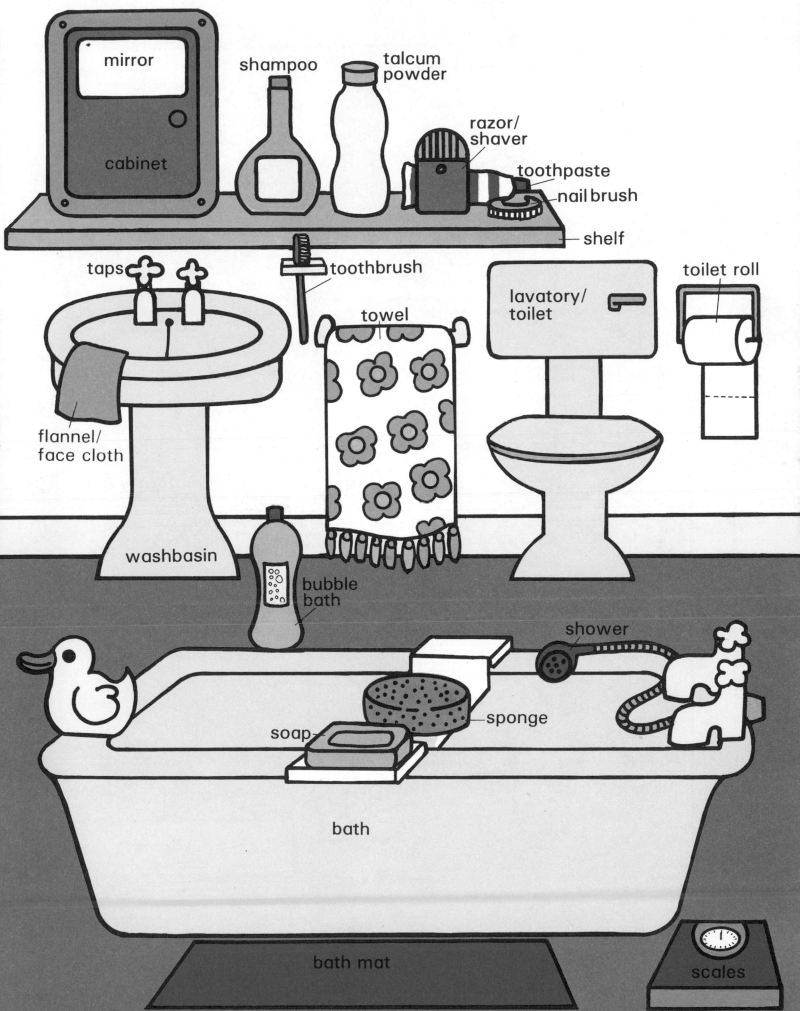

mirror

shampoo

talcum powder

razor/ shaver

toothpaste

nail brush

cabinet

shelf

taps

toothbrush

toilet roll

lavatory/ toilet

towel

flannel/ face cloth

washbasin

bubble bath

shower

sponge

soap

bath

bath mat

scales

13

Garden

clothes line/
washing line

bush

shed

hosepipe

spade

fork

hoe

rake

watering can

paddling pool

plants

seed box

ball

frog

lawn

stones

seeds

14

tree

greenhouse

tree

swing

compost/rubbish
heap

flower bed

lawn mower

wheelbarrow

soil/
earth

trowel

vegetables

plant pots

15

Car

fence

lawn

dustbin

garage

drive

windscreen

car seat

boot

petrol cap

steering wheel

bonnet

brake light

headlight

door handle

windscreen wipers

side light

indicator

bumper

hub cap

door

CAR 123

number plate

tyre

wheel

16

Tool shed

tool box

work bench

ladder

broom/brush

oil can

glue pot

file

chisel

screwdriver

screws

pliers

plane

hammer

nails

pincers

spanner

drill

electric
drill

axe

saw

Park/Playground

flowers

fountain

path

newspaper

bench

grass

litter bin

man

lead

dog

pond

duck

yacht

hedge

kite

railings

rocking horse

swing

see-saw

slide

roundabout

bucket

spade

sandpit

19

Street

garage

public house/pub

newsagent and sweetshop

petrol pump

litter bin

motor cycle

fish shop

greengrocer

book shop

town hall

car

yellow line

road

bus

hardware shop

jeweller

supermarket

butcher

IN

OUT

The Green Apple

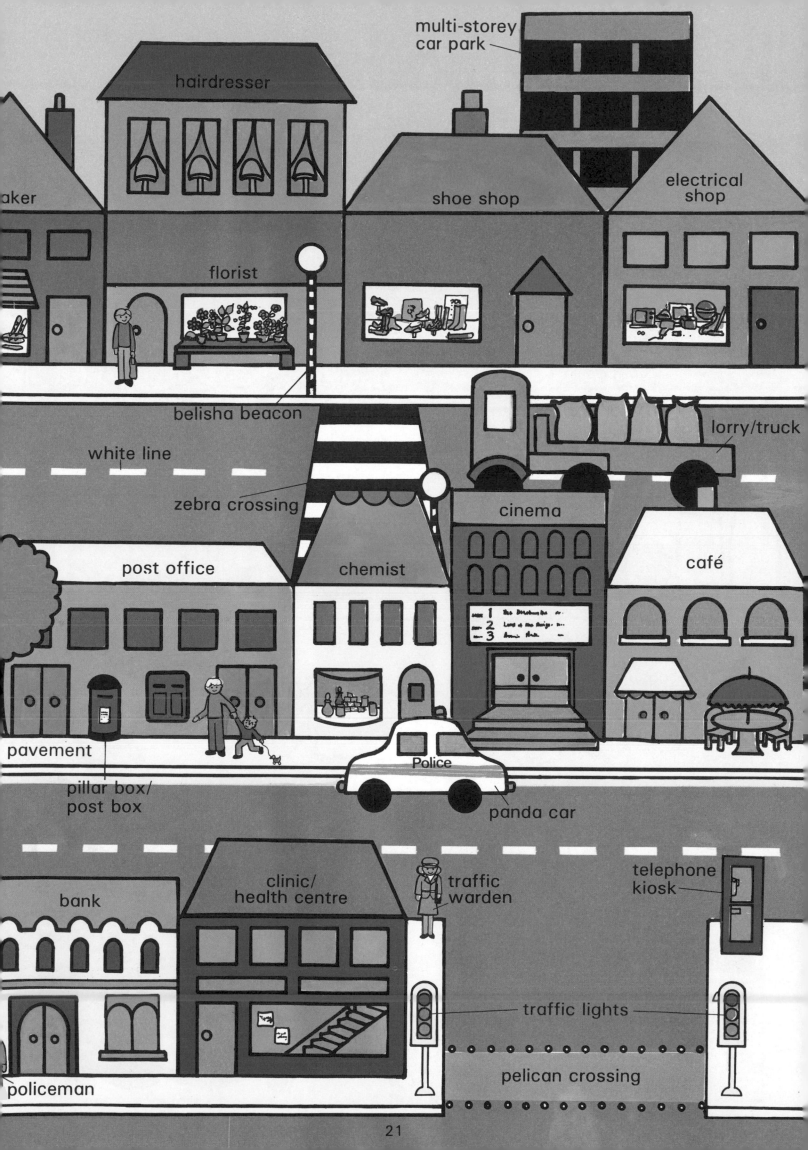

multi-storey
car park

hairdresser

electrical
shop

shoe shop

aker

florist

belisha beacon

lorry/truck

white line

zebra crossing

cinema

café

post office

chemist

1 ___
2 ___
3 ___

pavement

pillar box/
post box

Police

panda car

bank

clinic/
health centre

traffic
warden

telephone
kiosk

traffic lights

policeman

pelican crossing

Supermarket

drinks

wine

orange juice

tea

coffee

soup

flour

baked beans

milk

margarine

cream

butter

cheese

fish

chicken

yogurt

cashier

money

cash till

customer

chocolate

sweets

crisps

wire basket

trolley

bread
spaghetti
biscuits
cereal
cakes

jam
sugar
honey
soap powder
washing-up liquid
bleach
sauce
marmalade

meat
sausages
eggs
salad
lettuce
tomatoes
cucumbers
cress
celery
bacon

vegetables
cabbage
carrots
onions
mushrooms
peas
beans
potatoes
cauliflower

fruit
ranges
apples
strawberries
bananas
pears
raspberries
plums
grapes
lemons

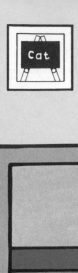

School

clock

book corner

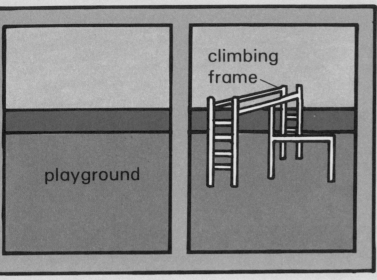
playground

climbing frame

milk bottles

girl reading

ball

p.e. apparatus

boy singing

hoop

beanbag

skipping rope

children dancing

blackboard

2 -

3 -

mathematics/sums/
number

chalk

pictures

desk

register

pen

ruler

teacher

waste
paper
bin

building
bricks

painting

paintbrush

pencil

paper

scissors

writing

jigsaw

crayons

drawing

glue

Hospital

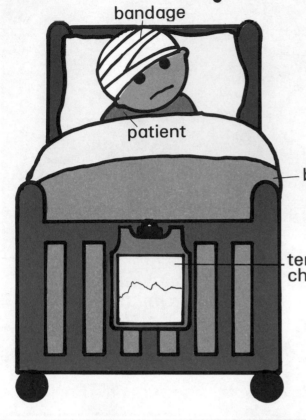

bandage

patient

bed

temperature chart

doctor

nurse

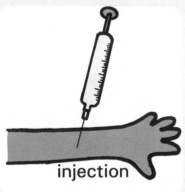
injection

ambulance

porter

wheel-chair

stethoscope

trolley

plaster

thermometer

stitches

operating theatre

surgeon

operation

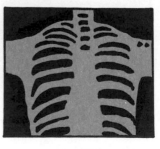
medicine   pills

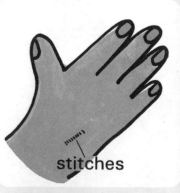
x-ray

Dentist

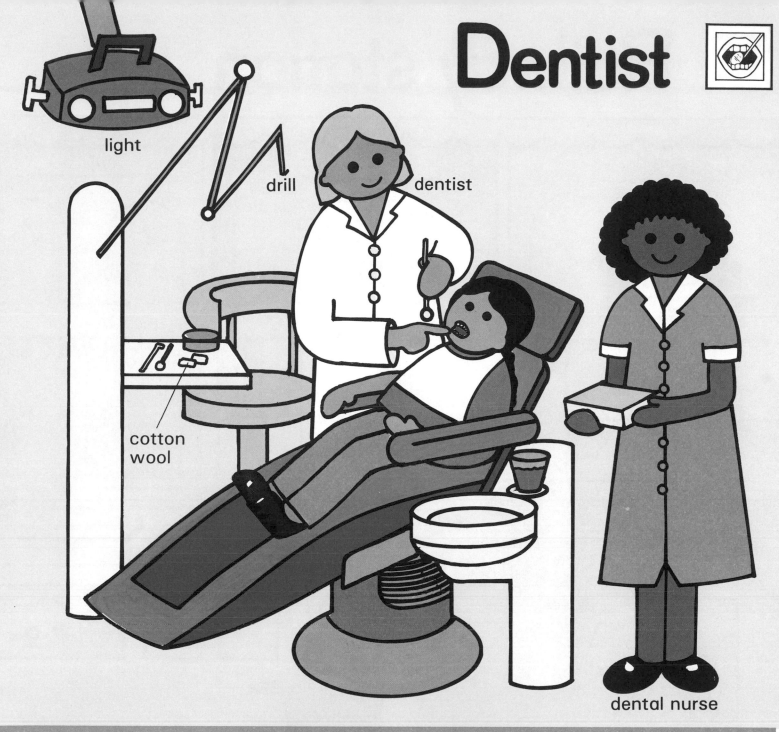

light

drill

dentist

cotton wool

dental nurse

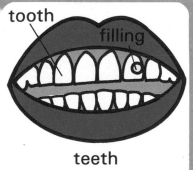

tooth

filling

teeth

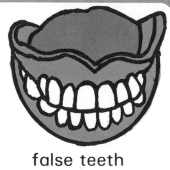

false teeth

mouthwash

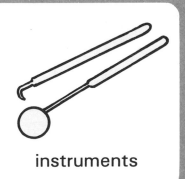

instruments

chair

waiting room

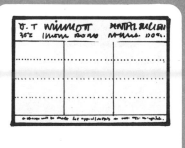

appointment card

receptionist

Railway station

buffet

waiting room

toilets

ladies

gentlemen

guards van

goods train

railway line

diesel engine

dining car

green flag

parcel

mailbag

suitcase

trolley

luggage

guard

platform

ticket office

porter

timetable

arrival

departure

28

Bus station

booking office

snack bar

ticket

conductor

coach

wheel

bus stop

pay as you enter

single-decker bus

driver

bus fare

handbag

briefcase

basket

passengers

29

Docks

lighthouse

hovercraft

funnel

tugboat

deck

cabin

ship

harbour

tanker

mast

cargo

cargo ship

crane

rope

anchor

sailor

captain

quay

Airport

wing

aeroplane

control tower

helicopter

runway

customs

cockpit

fuselage

tail

steps

pipe

fuel tanker

air stewardess

air steward

pilot

mechanic

radar scanner

31

Countryside

cloud

windmill

wood

hill

stream

lake

farmhouse

road

hay

farmer

lane

pig

hens

ducks

pond

farmyard

sheep

lamb

flowers

motorway

hedge

nest

scarecrow

tractor

field

plough

bridge

bull

goat

river

tree

cow

calf

stile

33

Seaside

seagull

sunshade/ umbrella

wind break

deck chair

beach bag

air bed

sunglasses

beach ball

towel

swimming trunks

swimming costume

rubber ring

rock

rock pool

crab

seaweed

icecream van

sun

donkey rides

steps

spade

promenade

bikini

sandcastle

donkey

bucket

beach

shell

wave

starfish

sea

shrimp

fish

lobster

pebbles

35

Zoo

cage

monkey

lion

hippopotamus

parrot

elephant

crocodile

polar bear

zoo keeper

seal

36

tiger

snake

kangaroo

zebra

rhinoceros

giraffe

dolphin

pelican

penguin

Funfair

big dipper

roundabout/
merry-go-round

waltzer

ghost train

Ghost

balloons

hot dog

Hot Dogs & Hamburgers

hamburger

big wheel

helter-skelter

side-shows

dodgems

coconut shy

rifle range

candy
floss

toffee
apple

popcorn

39

Circus

band

trapeze

trapeze artist

acrobat

lion

strongman

ringmaster

circus ring

seal

40

Big Top/circus tent

tightrope walker

performing dogs

audience

elephant

ballerina

juggling

clown

horse

Musical instruments

violin

bow

notes

electric guitar

guitar

double bass

banjo

piano

harp

maracas

steel drum

zither

trumpet

tuba

french horn

flute

recorder

trombone

drum

triangle

bongo drum

castanets

cymbals

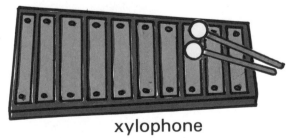

tambourine

xylophone

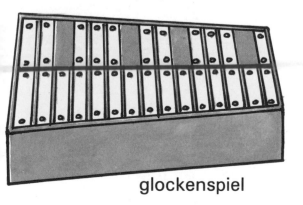

glockenspiel

conductor   orchestra

baton

music

Jobs

chef/cook

waiter/waitress

engineer

dustman

teacher

milkman

miner

hairdresser

factory worker

shop assistant

fireman

lorry driver/van driver

doctor

nurse

postman/postwoman

butcher

policeman/policewoman

scientist

Sports

swimming

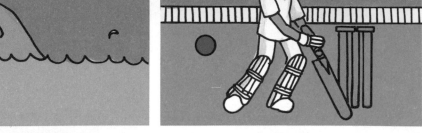
cricket

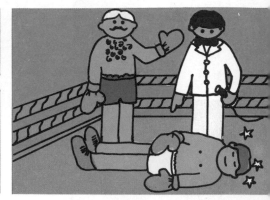
boxing

motor racing

skiing

golf

tennis

sailing

ice skating

show jumping

football

fishing

46

motor cycle racing

wrestling

rowing

running

badminton

hang gliding

rugby

netball

snooker

wind surfing

jumping

cycling

parachuting

47 hockey

table tennis

Small creatures

grasshopper

spider's web

moth

fly

caterpillar

ant

bee

earwig

mosquito

butterfly

spider

tadpole

centipede

wasp

slug

daddy-long-legs

ladybird

dragonfly

beetle

snail

worm

Flowers

sunflower

foxglove dahlia rose

snowdrop daffodil lupin tulip pansy crocus

poppy

bluebell dandelion daisy violet buttercup forget-me-not

Pets

budgerigar

dog

puppy

hamster

pony

mouse

rabbit

gerbil

guinea pig

tortoise

goldfish

kitten

cat

Birds

cockerel

chick

hen

duck

duckling

turkey

goose

gosling

swallow

sparrow

crow

robin

blue tit

blackbird

pigeon

thrush

starling

wren

owl

swan

cygnet

flamingo

eagle

51

Numbers

one elephant

two cars

three fish

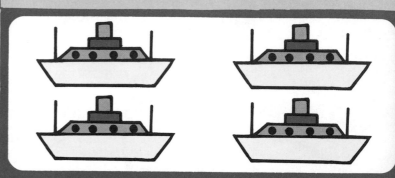

four ships

five drums

six toadstools

seven apples

eight birds

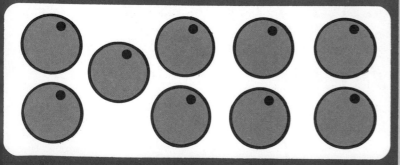

nine beads

ten ants

Shapes and colours

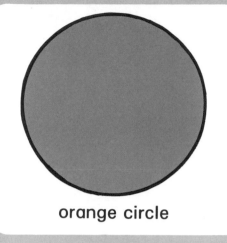

orange circle

black star

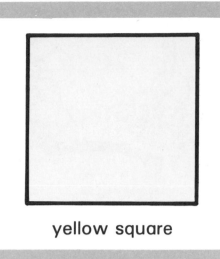

yellow square

purple diamond

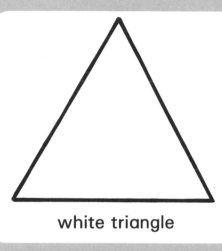

white triangle

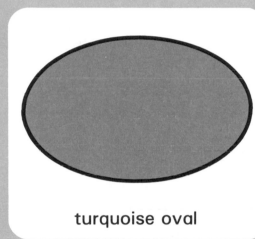

turquoise oval

brown cone

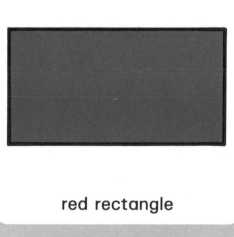

red rectangle

pink cube

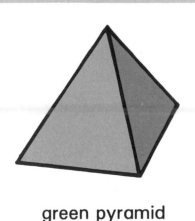

green pyramid

blue heart

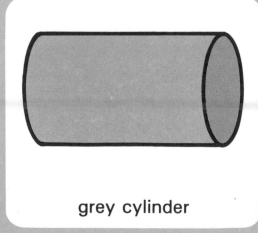

grey cylinder

Days of the week

Monday

Monday's child is fair of face

Tuesday

Tuesday's child is full of grace

Wednesday

Wednesday's child is full of woe

Thursday

Thursday's child has far to go

Friday

Friday's child is loving and giving

Saturday

Saturday's child works hard for a living

Sunday

but the child that is born on the Sabbath day is bonny and blithe and good and gay

Times of day

quarter to seven

dawn – sunrise

time to get up

eight o'clock

morning

time for breakfast

twelve o'clock

midday

time for lunch/dinner

half past three

afternoon

time for tea

six o'clock

dusk – evening

time for supper

quarter past eight

night

time for bed

Months of the year
January
February
March
April
May
June
July
August
September
October
November
December

Seasons

Some places have four seasons

warm

spring

hot

summer

cool

autumn

cold

winter

Some places have two seasons

wet season

dry season

Weather

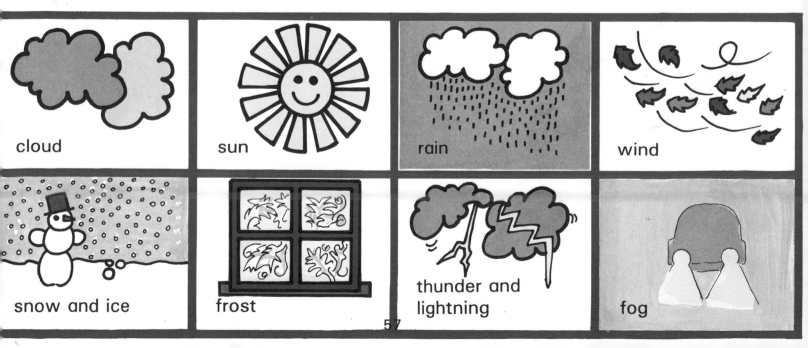

cloud

sun

rain

wind

snow and ice

frost

thunder and lightning

fog